Cape Disappointment

by Hannah Bos & Paul Thureen

Developed by Oliver Butler

A SAMUEL FRENCH ACTING EDITION

SAMUELFRENCH.COM
SAMUELFRENCH-LONDON.CO.UK

FOR PRODUCTION ENQUIRIES

UNITED STATES AND CANADA
Info@SamuelFrench.com
1-866-598-8449

UNITED KINGDOM AND EUROPE
Theatre@SamuelFrench-London.co.uk
020-7255-4302

Each title is subject to availability from Samuel French, depending upon country of performance. Please be aware that *CAPE DISAPPOINTMENT* may not be licensed by Samuel French in your territory. Professional and amateur producers should contact the nearest Samuel French office or licensing partner to verify availability.

MUSIC USE NOTE

Licensees are solely responsible for obtaining formal written permission from copyright owners to use copyrighted music in the performance of this play and are strongly cautioned to do so. If no such permission is obtained by the licensee, then the licensee must use only original music that the licensee owns and controls. Licensees are solely responsible and liable for all music clearances and shall indemnify the copyright owners of the play(s) and their licensing agent, Samuel French, against any costs, expenses, losses and liabilities arising from the use of music by licensees. Please contact the appropriate music licensing authority in your territory for the rights to any incidental music.

IMPORTANT BILLING AND CREDIT REQUIREMENTS

If you have obtained performance rights to this title, please refer to your licensing agreement for important billing and credit requirements.

CAPE DISAPPOINTMENT was first produced by The Debate Society at Performance Space 122 in New York City in November 2008, with scenic design by Karl Allen, lighting design by Mike Riggs, sound design and original music by Nathan Leigh, costume design by Sydney Maresca, projection design and editing by Casimir Nozkowski, animation by Tony Candelaria and Stef Choi, and voice-overs by Hal Douglas and Brian Grosz. Stage management was by Hope Bowman, with assistant stage management by Shelley Miles. The original set concept was developed by Amanda Rehbein and The Debate Society. It was directed by Oliver Butler. The cast was as follows:

FEMALE 1 . . . . Hannah Bos

FEMALE 2 . . . . Pamela Payton-Wright

MALE 1 . . . . Paul Thureen

MALE 2 . . . . Michael Cyril Creighton

CAPE DISAPPOINTMENT was developed with the support of chashama, the CUNY Prelude Festival, Dixon Place and The Fusebox Festival and made possible in part by grants from The Greenwall Foundation, The Puffin Foundation, The Mancini Foundation, and public funds from the Fund for Creative Communities, supported by the New York Stage Council on the Arts and administered by the Lower Manhattan Cultural Council. Gilda's Club served as a community sponsor for the premiere production.

CHARACTERS

Four Actors play all of the roles:

FEMALE 1 - Hannah, Mary, Little Girl, Mavis
FEMALE 2 - One-Arm, Aunt Gracie, Make-Up Lady
MALE 1 - Paul, Pedophile, Evert, MC
MALE 2 - Jack, Russell, Florence, Movie Theater Guy

NOTES ON *CAPE DISAPPOINTMENT*

At various points throughout the play we have indicated "Driving Interludes". During these sections we manipulated miniature cars with headlights across the dark landscape (like a wide shot in a film). These sections served to cover time for costume changes while also throwing in some cinematic visual vocabulary. You are welcome to fill the time as needed with sound or visual story.

- The Debate Society

(Preshow – Sunset, Fireflies)

(Highway sounds are heard far in the distance. Crickets. One or two fireflies. Dark. The stage is an old abandoned drive-in movie theater. Drive-in speakers are scattered throughout the audience, dangling on their posts, wires cut and frayed.)

Detroit

(A mini-play before the "feature".)

(PAUL *(very tall) and* **HANNAH** *(very short) stand side by side. Stationary. Never quite looking at each other. They are dressed early 20th century fancy.)*

PAUL. Detroit is our hometown!

HANNAH. And we love it!

PAUL. We sure know a lotta things about Detroit.

HANNAH. The best way to see Detroit is in a hot air balloon I'd think.

PAUL. Some facts about Detroit.

HANNAH. Twelve American presidents are buried in Detroit.

PAUL. There have been more World's Fairs in Detroit than any other city.

HANNAH. Detroit is the birthplace of those sensational Robinson Quints.

PAUL. In 1873 a severe cholera outbreak decimated London mere months after a typhoon washed away half of Peking. For the two years following, Detroit was the world's most populous city.

HANNAH. Detroit has some of the tallest buildings in the world.

PAUL. *(flirty)* But the smaller ones are known for their beauty and elegance.

HANNAH. *(blushing)* Well, I don't know about that –

PAUL. As many know, the city of Detroit radiates in concentric circles from a central lake. Though almost perfectly round, it is a natural lake and on still and sunny days hot air balloonists enjoy congregating over the lake and looking down at their reflections.

HANNAH. They call the lake, Mirror Lake.

PAUL. Well, that's just our nickname for it.

HANNAH. But maybe they call it that too.

PAUL. Yeah. Electromagnetism was invented in Detroit.

HANNAH. Cars too. I like hot air balloons.

PAUL. The streets became so crowded with speeding automobiles that pleasure-walkers feared being smeared alongside the stone buildings.

HANNAH. The car is king in Detroit.

PAUL. Ooo…Detroit is a city of slogans.

HANNAH. "Detroit: The city of windows."

PAUL. "Detroit: Where people are FROM."

HANNAH. "Detroit: Where I live."

PAUL. "Detroit: It's a city!"

HANNAH. "Hot Dog…Detroit!"

PAUL. It has been said that Detroit has so many slogans that if they were placed end to end –

HANNAH. Oh!…"Detroit: You said it!"

PAUL. "Detroit: It takes one to know one!"

HANNAH. "Dolphins love it. Welcome to Detroit!"

PAUL. "Guess where you are…Detroit!"

HANNAH. "Detroit: Taste It!"

PAUL. *(overlapping)* "Detroit: When you're here, you're in Detroit", "The City of Cities", "Detroit: Where people go", "The Boyhood Home of Mark Twain", "You'll know you are in Detroit when you get here", "Detroit: Our Days Are Numbered", "Yer in Detroit", "Try Detroit", "Detroit: Try It", "Welcome to Detroit".

HANNAH. *(overlapping)* "Detroit, where cars and stars are born", "Detroit: The little Great Britain", "Welcome to Detroit", "I'll See You In Detroit", "The Watch Capital of Tomorrow", "It's Detroit!", "I try Detroit", "Detroit: the city of people who try", "Home of Beth the Duck".

HANNAH. *(pause)* Tell me about the "Sweetheart Package".

PAUL. Well – on the outskirts of the city, engaged couples would put on their suits and dresses and take to the sky in hot air balloons. One thousand feet above the forests they would be married. Sometimes the sky was just full of wedding parties. When the ceremony was finished and their ride was complete, they would find a nearby field to land in and celebrate with a picnic and dancing amongst the sugar beets. An extra bottle of champagne was provided to smooth things over with irritated farmers.

HANNAH. "Brides 'n' Grooms in Hot Air Balloons". *(singing)* Brides…Mmmm…Bri-briiiiiides…

(**PAUL** *puts finger to ear and starts humming, trying to find the right tone. He joins in and together they sing "Brides 'n' Grooms in Hot Air Balloons". Then, maybe, they sing it a second time.)*

HANNAH & PAUL.

BRIDES 'N' GROOMS IN HOT AIR BALLOONS
SWINGING HIGH ALL AFTERNOON.
SHOULDN'T WE, COULDN'T WE, I AIN'T GOING BACK
'TIL YOU KISS ME.

HANNAH. Oh, I *loved* the Detroit Metropolitan Symphony.

PAUL. You know they used to say that many of Detroit's children were a result of their weekly live radio broadcasts. *(Slow smiles. This is as scandalous as it gets for them.)*

HANNAH. Back then that was the only program there was in Detroit.

PAUL. *But* if the evening was perfectly clear we might be lucky enough to catch a hint of a broadcast coming in from a far off place like…Los Angeles. *(pronounced old-timey exotic: "Lohs An-Ga-Leez")*

HANNAH. Or Elkhart.

(Recording of radio program begins. They listen.)

RECORDING. From Hollywood. Barry Sullivan in… *(static).* And now Mr. Barry Sullivan, outstanding motion picture and stage star in a drama of *The Unexpected*, titled: *Mercy Killing. (voice of another radio performer)* My name is Arnold Stanton. I've been married for twelve years. All our friends say that Evelyn and I are an ideal couple, devoted to each other. But a few minutes ago as I came through the front door…I decided to murder my wife.

(As music swells, it fades into static. **HANNAH** *and* **PAUL** *sway to pick up a signal, but to no avail. The static fades. They stand in silence.)*

HANNAH. Wait, what happened?

PAUL. Remember, that's when the clouds rolled in. We didn't hear the rest.

HANNAH. "Detroit: The city of bridges."

PAUL. "Detroit: When you're here, you're in Detroit!"

(Things slow down after this point. And get quieter. Lights begin to fade revealing tiny lit windows all over Hannah and Paul's costumes. They are buildings.)

HANNAH. Tell me where the bridges were.

PAUL. Detroit: Where every –

HANNAH. All the buildings are empty.

PAUL. Detroit:…

(At this point they are still and inaudible. Their mouths still move. Hot-air balloons drift across the stage.)

The Drive-In Slowly Starts to Come Alive

(silence)

(A faint bit of static comes through two or three speakers. Then more static with a little bit of ghostly language. Possibly:)

AUNT GRACIE. They'll never forget you, Florence.

(sound cuts out)

(silence)

(The Drive-In sign turns on and off with sounds of electricity being fed to it.)

(Speakers in the house pop and crackle.)

(In the dark, coming out of all the speakers, we hear:)

VOICEOVER. Ladies and Gentlemen. Welcome to the show. For the comfort and convenience of our patrons we hope you'll refrain from loud talking and roughhousing, turn off your headlights and anything else that will disturb the other patrons, and keep an eye on your children. Now please sit back, relax, refrain from loud talking and roughhousing...and enjoy our Feature Presentation.

Peacock

(A beautiful peacock emerges from behind the fence. It spreads its glorious feathers. A gunshot blows its head off.)

Pedophile – Flash of Solo Drive

*(Quick cut to the **PEDOPHILE** driving through the night. He has a bloody gauze eye patch. He's listening to the baseball game. The lights flicker like a ghost or film. Or a ghost film.)*

Brother and Sister – Run Out of Gas

*(JACK and MARY drive and listen to music. JACK is
behind the wheel.)*

JACK. Mother packed us sandwiches.

MARY. I know.

JACK. You want one?

MARY. No thank you.

JACK. Can you fetch one for me?

MARY. Sure.

JACK. You keeping an eye out for the turn-off?

MARY. Yes. There's that windmill right before the turn.

> *(She unwraps a sandwich and hands it to him. He takes
> a bite.)*

JACK. Sorta tastes off to me.

MARY. Just eat the bread then and the mustard. You can
pick something up at the train station.

> *(JACK hands the sandwich back to MARY.)*

JACK. Oh! Did I tell ya the swell news about Tommy
Wheeler?

MARY. No.

JACK. He broke both his wrist and his right leg!

MARY. Golly, Jack that's terrible.

JACK. Well, gee, it is but it isn't too. He was climbing near
the quarry and just started showing off and fell. I think
Eleanor and Charlotte were there.

MARY. Eleanor and Charlotte were there?

JACK. Yeah, anyways turns out –

MARY. Jack, roll up your window a little.

JACK. So it turns out he's out for the whole summer. So,
now I'm Mr. Dobbs' right hand man at the Five and
Dime! I get to do all the inventory and the back to
school sale. I'm gonna make loads with all those
hours, Mary.

MARY. Well that *is* swell, Jack. You can finally pay me back the two bucks you owe me.

JACK. Wait a second, Mary. I thought you knocked off a quarter cause I didn't tell Mom about that…thing.

(silence)

MARY. Oh, yeah. We did work that out, didn't we? So, we're down to one dollar and seventy-five cents. *(noticing a billboard)* Gee, there's another one! *(sings slogan)* "When yer in a pickle, sprinkle it on,"

MARY & JACK. *(unison)* "Dill's Talcum."

MARY. Mother is making me a dress based on that magazine photo of Betty Daphornie. Where she's in that last scene with the dying lamb in *Never Say Ever*. She's so graceful and elegant. Course my dress is going to be made from Thelma's winter curtains. They have a little sun damage but not too bad. Mother picked up some –

JACK. They say Aunt Gracie is a loony now, huh?

MARY. That's not a very nice thing to say, Jack.

JACK. Well it's true Mary. Dad said her mind's gone. That should make the ride back home a real thrill.

MARY. She used to be so funny when we were little. It's just so sad.

JACK. Sounds like she's a different kind of funny now.

*(**MARY** turns off radio.)*

MARY. Oh Jack, I wish you wouldn't say things like that.

(They drive in silence for a while.)

JACK. I wonder if that's going to happen to Mother.

MARY. Jack! She's much older than Mother.

JACK. I guess.

(pause)

JACK. Do you think you'll recognize her?

MARY. Of course! Don't you?

JACK. Sure, I guess.

MARY. Hey! Do you remember when Aunt Gracie used to tell us that story about the crazed gorilla and you would get so scared.

JACK. I wasn't really scared.

MARY. You cried every time, Jack.

JACK. No I didn't.

MARY. Jack!

JACK. Ok, maybe I cried once.

MARY. *(quick inhale)* Oh, I think that was the turn-off.

JACK. You sure?

MARY. I think so.

JACK. Golly Mary, I told you to keep an eye out.

MARY. Sorry Jack. Just turn around up here and we'll go back. Don't worry we have plenty of time.

(He turns the car.)

MARY. It's so dark already.

JACK. Yep.

MARY. Here we are…

JACK. So turn left here?

MARY. …Well now, I'm not sure. There's a windmill, but there was supposed to be a sign for the train station too.

JACK. Jeepers, this doesn't look right. Darn it. *(engine sputters)*

MARY. Jack! It's fine. We have plenty of time. Aunt Gracie's train isn't due – *(engine sputters)* What was that?

JACK. No! Look at the gas gauge! We need to find a service station quick. God-damn-it!

MARY. *(shocked inhale)*

Driving Interlude – Evert and Russell

(A model of **JACK** *and* **MARY***'s car drives off. From the other side of the stage, headlights from a model of* **EVERT** *and* **RUSSELL***'s truck emerge in the distance. Sound of truck engine and faint singing.)*

Evert and Russell – Singing. One Dragonfly.

(**RUSSELL** *and* **EVERT** *driving at night, singing the song on the radio, "When I Get Too Old to Dream ".** Their "truck" is the old ticket-booth, now somehow sporting headlights which point toward the audience.* **EVERT** *is at the wheel.*)

(*Cut to: later in the night. They are singing another song together.*)

(*Cut to:* **EVERT** *is singing and* **RUSSELL** *is asleep.*)

(*Cut to:*)

RUSSELL. But there's nothing wrong with my hardwood floor.

EVERT. Well certainly your old flooring has given you a lot of pleasure and service. You are thoroughly familiar with its condition and I can understand why you feel that it is sufficient. But, Mr. Prospect, I don't think I'd be able to sleep tonight if I didn't feel I'd done my utmost to inform you of the new features of comfort and safety that science has brought into existence since you last made a home-flooring investment.

RUSSELL. Science?

EVERT. Yes, Science! Our new linoleum floor coverings provide features that cannot be duplicated through any other processes...features that, if you care about the well-being of your family, you'd happily give up your trusty hardwood friend to obtain. Let me ask you a difficult question: can you be certain your family can remain happy and healthy given your current flooring situation?

RUSSELL. Ahhhh, the devil doubt.

EVERT. The devil doubt.

RUSSELL. The devil doubt gets 'em every time. Nicely done, very nicely done.

---

*See Music Use Note on page 3.

EVERT. Thank you.

RUSSELL. Now you do me.

EVERT. Ok…Uh…Sir, I lost my house in last week's catastrophic flood. So I have no floor to cover.

RUSSELL. Well, Mr. Prospect, I am sorry for your loss, but happily we are used to solving all sorts of flooring dilemmas. Why not start rebuilding your life from the ground up…with our new *water resistant* Aqua TruBlend 25. My partner and I can start installation next week, as soon as we get back from a little place you might have heard of called HOLLYWOOD!

(They yip with excitement.)

EVERT. Golly, I just can't wait!

RUSSELL. Me too.

EVERT. Are you up for just driving straight on through the night?

RUSSELL. Of course. That'll give us an extra day.

EVERT. Palm trees, coconuts…

RUSSELL. That'll be something!

EVERT. Oranges on a tree. That is something I've NEVER seen before. Can't wait to see that. Cabinet riding fine?

RUSSELL. *(looking out the back window)* Uh…she's looking good.

EVERT. You know what, tomorrow, if it's not too late after we unload, let's find someplace and take in a show?

RUSSELL. Yeah!?

EVERT. Why the hell not. You know, we should see that one –

(A huge dragonfly splats against the window.)

RUSSELL. Whoa. Look, a little dragonfly. Poor guy.

EVERT. Poor little thing. Here lemme –

(Switches on wipers. It smears like crazy.)

EVERT & RUSSELL. Ugh. Man. *(etc.)*

Driving Interlude – Pedophile

(Model of the **PEDOPHILE***'s car drives, baseball game on the radio. Car stops, hazard lights go on.)*

Pedophile – Second Solo Drive

(The **PEDOPHILE** *gets out of his car to smoke. He touches his bloody eyepatch. Headlights approach and he ducks into the darkness. He reappears, watches car drive off. Lights fade.)*

Brother and Sister – In the Woods

*(Stage is black. We can hear sticks snapping as **JACK** and **MARY** walk back to the car. She carries the flashlight and we can hear a gas can sloshing. They slap bugs. They walk for a while.)*

JACK. I can hardly see where I'm going.

MARY. Mother insisted that I wear these new shoes and now they are covered with mud.

JACK. Wash them off in the train station, Mary.

MARY. Ugh.

JACK. You're walking too fast.

MARY. I'm going slow.

(pause)

MARY. Do you think Eleanor and Charlotte are upset with me?

JACK. What?

MARY. Do you think Eleanor and Charlotte are upset with me? They never invite me to anything anymore.

JACK. Slow down, sis. I can't see back here.

MARY. I'm going slow.

(She turns and waits for him. He catches up and they walk side by side.)

MARY. I don't understand what Eleanor sees in Charlotte. Charlotte is such a show-off especially around boys and stuff. Are you spilling? It smells gassy.

(shines flashlight on him)

MARY. Jeepers, you got it all over yourself!

JACK. Darn it. The cap fell off. Gimme that.

*(He takes the flashlight and looks back over the path they came. He disappears into the trees. **MARY** is left alone in the dark. Long silence.)*

MARY. You find it?

> *(no answer)*

> Hey. You find it?

> *(nothing)*

> Jack? Jack? *(panicking)* Jack!

> *(He comes back.)*

JACK. There's no way I'm gonna find it out here.

MARY. Don't scare me like that!

JACK. I think if I stuff my hanky in here…

> *(He takes his hanky out of his pocket and stuffs it in the gas can hole.)*

JACK. That'll work. Here.

> *(gives the flashlight back to her)*

MARY. You know you'd better not smoke with all that stuff on you.

> *(flashlight flickers off)*

JACK. Hey sis, turn the light back on.

MARY. I'm trying. I think the switch is broken.

JACK. Just give it a little shake. Like this.

> *(**JACK** grabs the flashlight, shakes it, and it flickers back on.)*

JACK. There you go.

> *(They walk.)*

MARY. Golly, I gotta pee.

> *(They walk.)*

MARY. I really gotta pee.

JACK. Go pee then.

MARY. Light.

> *(He stays where he is and lights the way for her to go off and pee. She stops.)*

MARY. Turn it off.

(He does. Sound of pee on leaves. Then we can faintly hear the radio.)

MARY. Jeepers, do you hear that?

JACK. What?

MARY. Did we leave the radio on?

JACK. Guess so. Hope we start up ok. I know you don't like Charlotte, but I think she's nice. Eleanor can be a drag sometimes but that's just 'cause we've known her for so long. I think Charlotte is a breath of fresh air around here. Since she moved to town things have been real swell. Don't ya think?

(no answer)

Are you mad?

(no answer)

Come on Mary. Knock it off, sis. I know you're behind this…tree!

*(**JACK** shines the light where **MARY** was. She's gone.)*

Oh, Mary! Come on, we're already late, Aunt Gracie will be waiting.

(a creepy groan from deep in the woods)

Mary? I'm serious Mary. This isn't funny. Mary. Mary!!

*(Terrified, he runs through the woods frantically calling for **MARY**. Finally the beam of the flashlight lands on her.)*

JACK. There you are!

*(**MARY** stands completely still, looking up. She doesn't respond.)*

Mary? What?

(She points up into the trees. He turns to look. He whimpers. Flashlight goes out.)

Brother and Sister – Dirty Fright Drive

(**JACK** *and* **MARY** *are covered in dirt. They drive. They scream.*)

Evert and Russell – Hitting the Peacock

(The truck is parked at the side of the road. **EVERT** *and* **RUSSELL** *chat as* **EVERT** *finishes cleaning the dragonfly guts off the windshield.* **RUSSELL** *is peeing.)*

EVERT. *The Ruby of Cougar Isle?*

RUSSELL. Saw it last weekend.

EVERT. *Lady, He's Mine?*

RUSSELL. Saw it.

EVERT. Who's –

RUSSELL. Estelle Brethern.

EVERT. Estelle Brethern! That's right. I wanted to see that one. *The Lamplighter?*

RUSSELL. That's for kids.

EVERT. *Gypsy Eyes?*

RUSSELL. Yeah. But, I'd see that one again. Here, I'll do the next leg.

EVERT. Ok. I'll check the tarp.

*(***RUSSELL*** gets in the truck and starts up.* **EVERT** *hops in the passenger side. As the truck accelerates, the headlights brighten, blinding the audience, and suddenly switch to the red glow of tail lights.* **EVERT** *and* **RUSSELL** *have pivoted inside the "truck" so they now appear to be driving away from the audience instead of towards.)*

RUSSELL. *Gypsy Eyes* is something else. It really is.

EVERT. That so?

RUSSELL. That Eva Hayfield. There's just something about her. She just has the biggest eyes and there's this scene that's just…it's just heart breaking. She plays this – you know in real life her mother killed herself right in front of her. She put a knife in her throat.

EVERT. Oof.

RUSSELL. Anyway, there's another scene at the end –

EVERT. Don't give away the end!

RUSSELL. I'm not giving away the end. So near the end –

EVERT. Thank you.

RUSSELL. …there's this part…Eva Hayfield gets in a big fight with Lainie Fisher. You'd love it.

EVERT. Lainie Fisher's in the picture?

RUSSELL. Is she ever! So they're throwing vases, smashing paintings over each other's heads…then Eva Hayfield's poodle turns on the bathtub, so the whole room is filling with bubbles…Finally Lainie Fisher –

(Thump, they hit something. They stop the car and idle.)

EVERT. What was that?

RUSSELL. I think I just hit something.

(They look at each other. **EVERT** *rolls down his window. A frail woman appears suddenly in the headlights. She holds a rifle under her only arm. Where her other arm would be her sleeve is pinned up to keep it out of the way.)*

ONE-ARM. Oh Lord, oh Lord…

MAVIS. *(unseen)* MAMA!? Mama.

ONE-ARM. *(yelling off to the road side)* No Mavis, you stay back! Stay outta the road! *(turning back to the road)* Oh lord. He's dead. *(She crouches down and picks up a bloody peacock.)* Oh Christ almighty. What did you boys do? Gonna break Mavis's heart…she did love that bird. Like kin to Mavis. Yer blindin' me, shut them lights off! *(pause)* Shut 'em off!

(They turn off the lights, plunging stage into darkness.)

Get outta the truck.

Pedophile and Little Girl – First Drive

(The **PEDOPHILE** *drives, seemingly alone. He still has the bloody wad of gauze taped over one eye.* **LITTLE GIRL** *sits up in the back seat.)*

PEDOPHILE. Have a good sleep?

LITTLE GIRL. Mm-hm. Where are we?

PEDOPHILE. We'll be stopping soon. Next place we see.

(He drives, she looks out the window.)

LITTLE GIRL. I think I dreamed a knock-knock joke.

PEDOPHILE. Oh yeah?

LITTLE GIRL. Yeah. I don't remember how it goes though. Something about a giraffe.

PEDOPHILE. Was it funny?

LITTLE GIRL. They gave me a trophy for it, so I guess. *(pause)* Hey, did we win?

PEDOPHILE. I don't know. Lost the signal. We were up three-nil in the seventh so it looks pretty good.

LITTLE GIRL. Pretty Boy Mathers will find a way to lose it.

PEDOPHILE. You said it.

(He drives, she looks out the window.)

PEDOPHILE. Hey. What's your name?

LITTLE GIRL. I don't think I should tell you.

PEDOPHILE. Ok.

LITTLE GIRL. What's yours?

PEDOPHILE. Uh…I don't think I should tell you either.

NARRATOR. *(through drive-in speakers)* And with that, The Pedophile and The Little Girl drove off into the night.

*(***PEDOPHILE*** and* **LITTLE GIRL** *act out narration.)*

It had only been a few hours earlier that The Little Girl, sick and tired of her family's shouting and wrangling, had leapt into the family car, sped past her mother who was swinging a broom and her father who was kicking the dog, and turned out of her driveway, never to look back.

NARRATOR. *(cont.)* While the Little Girl was setting off on the open road, The Pedophile was spending *his* afternoon like he spent many afternoons: lying beneath the neighbor's floorboards, peering up at whatever happened to wander overhead.

TINY GIRL. *(voiceover)* Mama…There's an eyeball in the wood…There's an eyeball in the wood…Naw, it's not a knot…it's a eyeball… Blue eye's lookin at me…I'm coverin it up. With my finger. Gonna poke you in the eyeball!

(sound effect of finger squishing into Pedophile's eyeball)

NARRATOR. As afternoon turned into evening The Pedophile and The Little Girl both made their escapes…and that's how they met.

(Squealing tires. **LITTLE GIRL** *skids to a stop next to* **PEDOPHILE** *who is running and covering his injured eye with his hand. He turns and looks at her.)*

LITTLE GIRL. Hey Mister. Can you drive this thing? I can't see over the dash.

PEDOPHILE. Sure.

LITTLE GIRL. Well. Hop in then.

NARRATOR. The next morning the Pedophile and the Little Girl woke up early for their first full day together. They drove. They stopped to stretch. They drove some more.

PEDOPHILE. Hungry?

LITTLE GIRL. Almost.

(long pause)

PEDOPHILE. Any places you wanna see?

LITTLE GIRL. Mmmm… *(shrugs)*

(long pause)

LITTLE GIRL. It's really hilly.

PEDOPHILE. Oh yeah? That's because of the glaciers.

(drive for a while)

PEDOPHILE. Or is it that glaciers make things flat? Maybe that's what it is. I don't remember which.

LITTLE GIRL. Glaciers make things flat.

PEDOPHILE. That's right. We should stop somewhere and pick up some pamphlets. Then we can pick out where we want to go.

LITTLE GIRL. Neat. *(Quiet as she looks out the window for a while. They smell something.)*

PEDOPHILE. *(swerving the car)* Whoa.

LITTLE GIRL. *(turning to watch the roadkill disappear behind the car)* Ugghh.

PEDOPHILE. Ok, so you get two points for seeing a dead skunk or a dead squirrel. You get five points for a dead deer. And you get ten points for dead badger or any kind of squashed bird. Then we count up the points and see who wins.

LITTLE GIRL. Ok.

PEDOPHILE. Ok, go.

*(**PEDOPHILE** and **LITTLE GIRL** eagerly look out the windows. Lights fade. Lights dimly up on the car driving at night.)*

NARRATOR. On they drove, and as the days turned to weeks they went many places and saw many things. But…what neither The Pedophile nor the Little Girl remembered is that they had actually met once before: the previous spring when her parents hired him to clean out their gutters…

*(**PEDOPHILE** looks down at **LITTLE GIRL** as she scoops a piece of gum off the ground, wipes it off, and chews it.)*

PEDOPHILE. Did you just eat that off of the ground?

LITTLE GIRL. Yeah, what's it to you?

PEDOPHILE. Just saying ya could catch something.

LITTLE GIRL. What am I gunna catch, mister.

PEDOPHILE. Something bad. Nice bicycle.

LITTLE GIRL. She's alright.

PEDOPHILE. Where's your mamma?

LITTLE GIRL. Where's YOUR mamma?

NARRATOR. And so their story began.

Evert and Russell – Dinner

(**ONE-ARM** *chops potatoes with a hatchet then puts them on a grill made of old tires.* **MAVIS**, *a wild-looking girl, stands in the shadows. Bugs are buzzing. There is an old record player sitting on the ground. Also the headless, bloody peacock carcass. Sounds of crackling fire.*)

ONE-ARM. Mavis come sit by the fire, you gonna catch cold.

(**MAVIS** *walks closer, one leg dragging limply behind her.* **EVERT** *and* **RUSSELL** *emerge from the trees, carrying logs.*)

EVERT. Here you are ma'am. Will this be enough for you?

RUSSELL. Happy to find you some more.

ONE-ARM. Oh thank you Evert, thank you Russell, that's fine. This should do us for a while. Russell, could you move the bird over there by Mavis. I'm sure she'll want to say her goodbyes.

RUSSELL. Certainly.

(**MAVIS** *begins to sob.*)

RUSSELL. I want to apologize one more time, I just –

ONE-ARM. They had a special thing those two.

(*more crying*)

ONE-ARM. Don't cry, sugar snap.

EVERT. We feel terrible.

RUSSELL. We feel awful.

ONE-ARM. Seems tragic to meet you under such sad circumstances. You boys seem like such nice folks. I'll put a couple extra spuds on the fire. We don't get many visitors coming through these parts. Least you could do is be some company to us for an hour. Might be a comfort to Mavis.

EVERT. That is very generous. Oh certainly, we would love to stay for a bite.

ONE-ARM. Well then, go ahead and make yourselves comfortable.

(CUT TO:)

*(**MAVIS** is attaching record player to a car battery. **ONE-ARM** whispers to **EVERT** and **RUSSELL** by the fire.)*

ONE-ARM. She's virgin, ya know. And she has beautiful hair. Never. Been. Cut.

RUSSELL & EVERT. Lovely hair miss.

ONE-ARM. She's very good in the kitchen and with chores around the barn. Knows how to fix just about anything. Ya see Mavis's father, Emerson, he passed about two years ago. Shot himself in the face and then set fire to our house. Things just haven't been the same around here. She sulks and don't speak much but she takes excellent care of me and sometimes she makes jokes and stuff to keep our spirits high.

*(**MAVIS** gets shocked by the battery. Music starts playing.)*

ONE-ARM. She's a Sagittarius ya know.

MAVIS. I'm a Sagittarius.

RUSSELL. Is that so?

ONE-ARM. One of her foots is loppy though.

MAVIS. One of my foots is loppy though.

RUSSELL. I didn't even notice!

(CUT TO:)

EVERT. And he was really pleased with the new floor we put in for him. Turns out, he's been looking for someone to bring this china cabinet out west for him. Real nice heirloom thing. An oriental piece. Wants to give it as a gift to his daughter who's getting married out there. He didn't trust shippers with something that important. And well, we have a truck, so he asked us…and here we are. He's paying us a nice rate and gas…and we're just, well we're just having a high time of it. It's been a real treat.

ONE-ARM. Well isn't that something?

EVERT. We're gonna stay out there for a few extra days once we do the drop off. Russell's a tremendous motion picture buff and I'm excited about everything: the sunshine and the beach and all the fruit trees so…

(CUT TO:)

*(**RUSSELL** and **EVERT**, excitedly tag-team the story. **ONE-ARM** and **MAVIS** sit by the fire, enraptured.)*

RUSSELL. Doreen Wonderlick walks into a French café and there's this monkey dressed up in a little monkey sized tuxedo –

EVERT. And a top hat.

RUSSELL. And he runs up behind Howard Price who is playing the maître d –

EVERT. He's a terrific actor.

RUSSELL. He's good, real talented actor. So the monkey runs up on his shoulder-

EVERT. And in front of everybody –

RUSSELL. The monkey pulls off his toupee!

*(**ONE-ARM** laughs uncontrollably. It is otherworldly and lasts too long. The men join in but she continues. **MAVIS** joins in the fun when she sees her mother laughing.)*

ONE-ARM. Oh, Mavis loves monkeys! Mavis make that monkey sound.

MAVIS. No.

ONE-ARM. Make it.

MAVIS. *(obliging)* Oooh ohoh!

(CUT TO:)

*(**MAVIS** tap dancing. Working loppy foot with super long shoelaces. **EVERT** and **RUSSELL** whoop and clap.)*

(CUT TO:)

*(**ONE-ARM** finishing singing a mournful song. Everyone claps, moved.)*

ONE-ARM. Now Evert, if we're gonna keep this going all night, we're gonna need some more logs for the fire. Would you mind going to fetch some?

EVERT. It would be my pleasure. I'll be right back.

(*He exits into the trees.*)

ONE-ARM. Looking forward to it. Now, Russell, how about taking Mavis over for a peek at that china cabinet?

RUSSELL. I'd be happy to. Mavis?

(**RUSSELL** *and* **MAVIS** *exit towards truck.* **ONE-ARM** *picks up gun and follows.*)

One-Arm/Mavis/Russell – The Drive

(**RUSSELL**, *terrified and in his underwear, drives the truck.* **ONE-ARM** *points the gun at him with both arms and* **MAVIS** *looks on.*)

ONE-ARM. I'm gonna keep the truck. And I'm gonna keep that china cabinet. And Mavis is gonna keep your shirt.

(**MAVIS** *sniffs the shirt she's holding in her hands.*)

But as long as you get us out West, I ain't gonna hurt ya.

RUSSELL. Thank you ma'am.

(*blackout*)

Pedophile and Little Girl – Pit Stop

NARRATOR. The Pedophile and the Little Girl's adventure continued along many roads, over three covered bridges and around a big lake. They stopped at a llama ranch. It was closed. They climbed back in the car and continued on their way.

(lights up on day driving)

LITTLE GIRL. Look!

(They drive. She brushes her hair.)

LITTLE GIRL. Did you hear about that elephant that fell off that truck one time?

PEDOPHILE. No.

LITTLE GIRL. Yeah, this elephant that was working for the circus was on the back of a big truck and they were going to another town and the truck was going fast and the elephant fell onto the road and died.

PEDOPHILE. That's sad.

LITTLE GIRL. They got him off the road with water hoses. Let's pull over. I'm fiending.

PEDOPHILE. Already?

LITTLE GIRL. I need another one.

PEDOPHILE. We stopped an hour ago.

LITTLE GIRL. Just a quick one. Come on!

PEDOPHILE. All right.

LITTLE GIRL. Yes!

(They pull over.)

PEDOPHILE. Have at it.

(LITTLE GIRL drags her hula-hoop out of the back seat. He smokes, she hula-hoops. They laugh and talk.)

NARRATOR. And now I'll tell you what happens next:
The Pedophile shows The Little Girl a magic trick.
The Little Girl teaches The Pedophile to swim.
The Little Girl takes the wheel.

The Pedophile carves a duck.

The Pedophile and The Little Girl win a contest.

The Pedophile and The Little Girl see an Indian.

The Pedophile and The Little Girl sing a tune.

The Pedophile and The Little Girl retreat to the woods.

The Pedophile and The Little Girl light a fire.

The Pedophile and The Little Girl dine like kings.

The Pedophile and The Little Girl talk about tomorrow.

The Pedophile and The Little Girl see a picture.

The Pedophile and The Little Girl escape.

The Pedophile has a dream.

The Little Girl grows up.

The Pedophile and The Little Girl see the Ocean.

Brother and Sister – Aunt's Monologue/Crash

(Long silence as the three ride quietly. **MARY** *and* **JACK** *stare ahead in a daze.* **AUNT GRACIE** *sits between them.)*

*(***JACK*** turns on the radio.)*

AUNT GRACIE. Oh, thank you Jack.

(The three drive quietly.)

AUNT GRACIE. Jack. *(She stares at him, then:)* You look very dapper, Jack. *(looks back out the window, then over at* **MARY***)* Mary, do you have a boyfriend?

MARY. No.

AUNT GRACIE. I was just about your age when this new boy moved into our neighborhood. This was before we had to move away. The baby wasn't born yet – *(correcting herself)* your *mother* wasn't born yet, so you don't know this. I don't even know how to say it. It's not... don't worry, it's not bad.

(She stops talking and they drive quietly.)

JACK. Aunt Gracie, would you like to listen to some – *(He makes a move to turn on the radio and then realizes he already did.)* ...oh.

AUNT GRACIE. It's a state of mind that's all but lost now. Except for little children I guess. But even the children are different now. When I was a girl I wrote this little story called "The Candle", and it began, I don't remember most of it, I've lost it, but um, it began, "It was Christmas Eve, snow was covering all the ground and chimney tops, glistening with a silver brightness." I was ten or eleven when I wrote that. "The candle by my bedside began to flicker as many thoughts went though my mind," and I don't remember what those thoughts were. In the end "The candle flickered again and then went out." And...I don't know it was just this sense of...um, it was all dark except for the snow, and looking out it was quiet and I was alone in my room and anybody else was downstairs and...somehow it seemed...*remote.* Like we weren't in a village even. It was as if the whole world was holding its breath, waiting for something. And now I think about the wonder of how I loved that night. Sisterville was...it was a nothing place. It was nothing. You can't even describe it. It was ordinary and simple...But still it was...it was... This morning, I was trying to remember the last line I said in my scene at the pageant. "Watch over..." I can't remember it but it was about wishing comfort through the night...protecting us from harm...and I thought, my God...if someone had just said a prayer like that for Sisterville, if they could have seen what was coming...This sweet little place, you know. And then all of a sudden we felt we didn't have enough.

I was a very little girl then, but I remember it. One day somebody, and nobody remembers who it was, I don't. Maybe my father did, but...but anyway they got the idea to build a lake. Because if you had a lake, then there'd be all those other things that would go with it. A beach and a boardwalk. Waterskiing acrobats. And it would be a place people would flock to. That was what they were hoping. And in the end everyone thought that'd be great: people coming. And I was...well, probably when it started I was around seven because it went on for about ten years, the planning and the building. Everyone was so excited that last summer and I was caught up in it too. There was dancing every night and the parade and boats and paddle boats lined up like cars in parking lots, waiting to be launched. They were getting everything watertight and the whole town smelled of hot tar...and chocolate...and frankfurters. People were moving in from everywhere and I had so many new friends. Tilly and Mandy. We girls would run around the town and practice our walks. Tilly was so long and elegant, a real beauty. Mandy was plain but funny and I was the actress. Hmm.

And there were all these new boys and they were... sharp. That's what we called them. *Sharp.* They were so...exciting...and...They were different though, not like the boys raised in Sisterville. Those boys had old-fashioned manners. My father preferred them. And what happened was… *(stops herself and looks at* **MARY***)* Oh, I don't know. I can't…You grow up with funny ideas when you're innocent like that. I thought babies came out of the mouth, bassinet and all. Pink satin ribbons flying. I guess they don't.

Mary, you've got something on your face, dear.

Oh Jack, you'd be interested in this. People say there were problems with the Indians or they talk about that business with the mayor's wife and the County Assessor…but the real thing was the national shortage of three-way ball valves. That's all it was. You can't build a dam without those valves. So they never got the water to come. And that was that.

JACK. What's a three-way ball valve?

AUNT GRACIE. I don't know, but you can't build a dam without them.

Everyone left. The motel keepers and swim teachers. Things got very bad after that. Very bad. The suicides started. Civil engineers. Some lifeguards. Bobby. He was…he was a new boy in our neighborhood. That was so…Oh, you look so much like him, Jack.

He dove right off the new lighthouse, landing in the concrete lakebed.

I don't think I should tell you these things.

How are you Jack? How is school?

JACK. Good.

AUNT GRACIE. Hm. *(She looks at* **MARY** *for a while.)* Mary, you used to be younger. That's fine. *(pause)*

They put up a fake lake for a while…two-way mirrors and such. Just to keep spirits up and have something to look at. But people kept getting hurt and confused. They hung a neon moon off the side of the lighthouse. I thought that was sweet. It helped a little. Electric costs got high though. You don't think of that kind of thing. Sisterville Lighthouse is *still* the largest landlocked lighthouse in the world. So at least there's that.

I was crowned before all this happened. Do you remember that little crown I would let you wear when you would play dress up?

MARY. Oh yes!

AUNT GRACIE. That was my crown!

MARY. I remember. It was so pretty.

AUNT GRACIE. I was the very first Miss Sisterville! Well… There was only the one, so I'm still reigning queen I guess.

(They all laugh.)

JACK. How many girls did you beat?

AUNT GRACIE. Oh Jack! Well…I guess the month before the water was supposed to come they approached us all in school. And then pretty much any girl from town who owned both a dress and a bathing suit competed. You know to a young girl you say "beauty pageant", you know that's like "Oh!" Like that. It's fun.

*(**JACK** and **MARY** laugh.)*

I did my walk and wore my bathing suit and I performed the whole first act of *Nillie's Faerie Island* in three minutes.

JACK. In three minutes!

MARY. We loved that story!

AUNT GRACIE. I played all the parts, even the dog, and did the flying and everything. *"Timothy, someone's hiding in the cupboards." "Yes, yes, I can see it through the keyhole." "Is it her?…"*

*(**JACK** and **MARY** join in for the second part of the famous line…)*

ALL. "Could it be?"

AUNT GRACIE. *"Fanny, come quick and fetch me a broom! She's floating away!" "Woof, woof!" "And off I goooooo…"* (hearing a new song on the radio) Oh! I *love* this song…

(She turns up the volume on the radio and the three sing in unison.)

ALL. A you're adorable, B you're so beautiful, C you're a cutie full of charms. D you're –

(tires squeal)

(CRASH!!!!!!!)

(blackout)

(The sound of the crash settles. Silence. Then sounds of popcorn.)

Intermission Fake-Out

VOICEOVER. And now Ladies and Gentlemen…it's Intermission Time. Time for that stretch you've been waiting for. But before you get up, let me tell you about the scrumptious array of treats at the snack bar. Hungry? The popcorn's popping and buttery hot. Hotdogs made from the choicest franks and cooked till they're just right. The cold drinks are sparkling and there's all kinds of candy and your favorite cigarettes. Remember: babies get hungry too. Free bottle warmer service at the concession stand.

So…back to our Feature Presentation.

(Note: No intermission is actually taken.)

Sisterville Pageant

*(In the dark we hear recording of "A - You're Adorable"** *which morphs into a contestant,* **FLORENCE***, singing it terribly and twirling a baton as lights come up on the Miss Sisterville Pageant. The world has transformed into the glory days. Lights and sound…She finishes the song, curtsies, and begins to exit.)*

MC. That's fine, that's just fine. Thank you Florence.

*(***FLORENCE*** trips and falls while exiting.)*

Oop, careful now. Gee that was quite a fall. Now before we move on, I wanna remind you folks that today's festivities are brought to you by Sisterville Marina, the future home of what's surely to be Sisterville's largest watercraft fleet. "Be your need rowboats, paddleboats, showboats or houseboats you'll surely know where to find 'em."

So our sincere thanks to Sisterville Marina. *And* to Duffy's Life Preservers. Duffy says: "If you got a boat, you gotta have a Duffy's Life Preserver."

And now it's my pleasure to introduce this afternoon's final contestant, lovely Grace Mae Dalton, favoring us with a dramatic interpretation. Grace Mae Dalton!

(No one enters.)

Grace Mae Dalton!

(nope)

Grace Mae?

(exits looking for her)

MC. *(voice-over)* Hold tight folks while I find Grace Mae. Let's bring the Lovely Shelley Sisters back in to favor us with their sweet harmonies.

---

*See Music Use Note on page 3.

Pedophile and Little Girl – Crash Drive-By

(**PEDOPHILE** *drives at night,* **LITTLE GIRL** *sleeps, leaning on his shoulder. She wakes up, looks over at him and smiles. We hear sirens and see police flashers...* **PEDOPHILE** *decelerates as they pass between two crashed cars. We hear the songs that were playing in* **EVERT** *and* **RUSSELL***'s truck and* **JACK** *and* **MARY***'s car playing through mashed speakers. Music slows down, and we see* **LITTLE GIRL** *slowly turn. She waves out the window.)*

Sisterville II

(**AUNT GRACIE**, *back to audience, talks to* **FLORENCE.**)

AUNT GRACIE. Ya gotta keep your head up Florence. That was a beautiful rendition of a highly popular song. And you sounded swell. And most importantly ya finished with a bang! Ha. Right? They're not gonna forget you, Florence. See I see a smile under those tears.

MC. *(voice-over)* Grace Mae? Grace Mae?

AUNT GRACIE. Oh, that's me…oh…

(*They hug.*)

FLORENCE. Go get 'em Gracie!

(**AUNT GRACIE** *runs toward the stage and then turns to wave excitedly at* **FLORENCE.** *She takes the stage.*)

AUNT GRACIE. Good evening ladies and gentlemen. My name is Grace Mae Dalton. I was born right here in Sisterville and I am so happy to be here today.

Pedophile and Little Girl – Fireside/Drive-In

(PEDOPHILE and **LITTLE GIRL** *stand by a campfire. They hold tin cans and brush their teeth. They are looking at flyers and the* **LITTLE GIRL** *hands three to the* **PEDOPHILE**.*)*

LITTLE GIRL. First choice. Second choice. Third choice.

PEDOPHILE. What about the bottle house?

LITTLE GIRL. I didn't see that one.

PEDOPHILE. Wait…uh…there it is.

(He picks up a flyer from the ground.)

PEDOPHILE. See. It's that place that looks like a castle and it's made outta bottles and sea glass. They have a little museum there and when you stand inside the whole thing turns different colors. The owners passed away and –

LITTLE GIRL. What's…frog! There's a frog!

(They try to catch the frog until **PEDOPHILE** *spots a movie playing at a far away drive-in.)*

PEDOPHILE. Look! Look!

(They stand and look at the distant screen. An animation version of the Detroit prologue plays on the screen… "Brides 'n' Grooms In Hot Air Balloons" is faintly heard.)*

LITTLE GIRL. Can we go!?

PEDOPHILE. Yeah, sure.

(lights fade)

(The audience serves as cars at the drive-in and we hear the movie through their speakers. Soundscape surrounding audience in the theater: Cars creaking from making-out couples, popcorn crunching, etc. Maybe headlights come from a car, and a **MOVIE THEATER GUY** *tells them to turn them off.)*

---

*See Music Use Note on page 3.

(We see **PEDOPHILE** *and* **LITTLE GIRL** *on-stage sitting in a car seat watching the movie, backs to the audience. The voice of a woman speaking French is heard and subtitles are visible on the bottom of the screen above their heads. Subtitles end with:)*

(This music!
This wonderful, wonderful music!
Oh, would you just listen…
I love this music, Marie.)

*(***LITTLE GIRL** *turns and says something funny and they both laugh. They keep talking and laughing, pretty much ignoring the movie. A crash happens on screen, startling* **PEDOPHILE** *and* **LITTLE GIRL**. *They laugh. Soon we begin to hear their conversation over the drive-in speakers as the subtitles below are projected, unseen by* **PEDOPHILE** *and* **LITTLE GIRL**.*)*

(Subtitles:

I remember Thief's Caverns,
and that pretty bridge.
All those places we went.
The water is cool on my feet.
Salt water taffy!
We should build a house here.
What are you thinking?
Me too.
I have sand all over…
…in every little crevice.
Take me for a spin.
You make me feel dizzy.
You taste sweet.
You are my sweet.
You make a funny noise when you sleep.
Can we always do these things?
The summer is almost over.
I wish we could stay here.)

*(***PEDOPHILE/LITTLE GIRL** *conversation –)*

PEDOPHILE. *(voiceover)* Last night I had a dream that a parade of Campfire Girls came to take you away. But you didn't want to go. And then they sang you their song.

LITTLE GIRL. *(voiceover)* How did it go?

PEDOPHILE *(voiceover)* I don't remember, but it was about wanting to play with you and that you could brush each other's hair. Then they marched away. And you went with them. And I think one of them was your mother. And they all had oranges in their hands.

LITTLE GIRL. *(voiceover)* That's a funny dream. Where are we going to stay tomorrow night?

PEDOPHILE. *(voiceover)* I don't know. Where do you –

LITTLE GIRL. *(voiceover)* How about the teepees?

PEDOPHILE. *(voiceover)* Yeah?

LITTLE GIRL. *(voiceover)* Yes! We can sleep like settlers. Like we're on the wagon trail, and the teepee is our covered wagon and we're picking out where we're going to build our log house. And then we can pretend the teepee is our house and we can make rooms for everyone and decide where the kitchen is and where the kids sleep. And then… we can wake up together and eat bacon with maple syrup.

PEDOPHILE. *(voiceover)* Mm-hm.

LITTLE GIRL. *(voiceover)* And then…um…

PEDOPHILE. *(voiceover)* We won't be far from the water. We should drive there.

LITTLE GIRL. *(voiceover)* Yes! Can I tell you a secret?

PEDOPHILE. *(voiceover)* Mm-hm.

LITTLE GIRL. *(voiceover)* *(She sits there and grins at him.)* I'll tell you tomorrow.

PEDOPHILE. *(voiceover)* Ok. Maybe when we get to the ocean.

Pedophile and Little Girl – Little Girl Grows Up
(Costume Change)

*(**PEDOPHILE** and **LITTLE GIRL** "accelerate" out of the drive-in and into the night. As they drive, **MAKE-UP LADY** enters, as if onto the set of a film, and walks right up to their car, which continues to drive. It should look like a moment between a film takes, where the car driving effect continues, but the actors step out of character for the **LITTLE GIRL** to be transformed into a woman. **MAKE-UP LADY** adjusts **LITTLE GIRL**'s costume (making her look more grown up), ties her hair up and applies make-up. They talk quietly…almost inaudible to the audience.)*

MAKE-UP LADY. Turn towards me a little, hon.

LITTLE GIRL. Ok.

*(**MAKE-UP LADY** applies more makeup.)*

MAKE-UP LADY. Look down for me.

*(**LITTLE GIRL** tilts head down.)*

MAKE-UP LADY. Just with your eyes.

LITTLE GIRL. You smell nice.

MAKE-UP LADY. It's just Chantilly.

LITTLE GIRL. Can I see?

MAKE-UP LADY. Mm-hm *(holds up mirror)*

LITTLE GIRL. I like this color.

MAKE-UP LADY. And let me see *(**LITTLE GIRL** looks at **MAKE-UP LADY**.)* …Great.

*(**MAKE-UP LADY** begins to exit, but sees **LITTLE GIRL** is afraid. She comes back and kneels next to her.)*

MAKE-UP LADY. Everybody gets scared. But you'll be fine. It'll be great. You'll love it.

NARRATOR. The next day the Pedophile and the Little Girl woke up very early, eager and excited to take to the road. A fox ran –

*(**NARRATOR** stops, clears his throat, and begins again.)*

The next day the Pedophile and the Little Girl woke up very early, eager and excited to take to the road. A fox ran next to the car for a moment, just like a house-trained animal. They didn't notice. The leaves were starting to fall and The Pedophile and The Little Girl drove and drove until at last they came to the Ocean.

Pedophile and Little Girl – At the Lighthouse

(**LITTLE GIRL** *(now looking like a young woman) gets out of the car. They're at the coast. She looks out at the ocean.* **PEDOPHILE** *takes a breath and gets out of the car. He walks up behind her, happy and eager. They can be seen faintly in the moonlight, maybe silhouetted against a dark blue sky, and the beam of a lighthouse in the distance illuminates them each time it sweeps by.)*

PEDOPHILE. It's gonna be cold down there.

LITTLE GIRL. *(Her voice sounds a little older now.)* Oh yeah. I wasn't thinking we were gonna swim. Were you?

PEDOPHILE. I guess that's what I thought before.

(He looks at her, noticing something. She's different now? He fumbles for his cigarettes.)

LITTLE GIRL. What time is it?

PEDOPHILE. I dunno.

LITTLE GIRL. I'll have one of those.

PEDOPHILE. Mm-hm. *(He gives her one and lights it. They stand silently and smoke.)* There's a little zoo down there, by that carnival. I saw a flyer at the rest stop.

LITTLE GIRL. What?

(He doesn't answer. He's realizing it's over.)

It's pretty out here.

PEDOPHILE. Yeah.

(They stand and smoke.)

NARRATOR. The Pedophile and the Young Woman sat by the Ocean. And that was that.

(fade to black)

Finale

*(Lights fade up on **AUNT GRACIE** walking in a daze through the rubble of the crash. Red and blue police lights flash around her. We see bodies and steam and metal. **GRACIE** crouches by **JACK**'s lifeless body. She sees a car drive by and waves. She stands in the beam of a car headlight, then turns and comes downstage to face the audience.)*

AUNT GRACIE. Good evening Ladies and Gentlemen. My name is Grace Mae Dalton. I was born right here in Sisterville and I am so happy to be here today. I would like to thank the honorable Mayor Jefferson L. Simms, the city council and Sisterville Marina for today's celebration. When I grow up, I would like to be an actress. This evening, it is my pleasure to present for you, the first act of *Nillie's Faerie Island*. I will be performing all of the roles in just under three minutes. I hope you enjoy my performance of *Nillie's Faerie Island*. Thank you.

(She puts her head down. Collects herself. Then begins.)

"Night stars, as I leave my island home tonight, watch over my dear faerie friends. Keep them safe until I return, so they will grow to know that within their hearts there burns such a light as to brighten the whole earth."

(She closes her eyes. She lifts her arms, preparing to fly…)

THE END

ACKNOWLEDGEMENTS

A special thanks to: Eileen Casterline, Rachel Levens, Hanlon Smith-Dorsey, Amy Ehrenberg, Sarah Lazarus, Ian Savage, Gilda's Club, Rob Reddy, Risa Shoup, Amy Rose Marsh, Amanda Rehbein, Casimir Nozkowski, Matt Elkind, Ron Berry, Natalie George, Cyndi Williams, Leslie Strongwater, Andy Horwitz, Sarah Douglas, Charlene Bos, Manbites Dog Theater, Vallejo Gantner and the PS122 staff & crew.